Motor Goose

Rhymes That Go!

In memory of my cousin Johnny B, a master of motors.—R.C.

For my dad—who taught me to love cars. Especially E-Types.
For my mom—who loves art. Specifically mine.
And for Edna Schmedna—who taught me that Little Piggies sometimes go
to market, stay home, have roast beef, or go "wee, wee, wee" all the way home!—J.K.

A FEIWEL AND FRIENDS Book
An imprint of Macmillan Publishing Group, LLC

Motor Goose. Text copyright © 2017 by Rebecca Colby. Illustrations copyright © 2017 by Jef Kaminsky.
All rights reserved. Printed in China by RR Donnelley Asia Printing Solutions Ltd., Dongguan City, Guangdong Province.
For information, address Feiwel and Friends, 175 Fifth Avenue, New York, N.Y. 10010.

Our books may be purchased in bulk for promotional, educational, or business use.
Please contact your local bookseller or the Macmillan Corporate and Premium Sales Department at
(800) 221-7945 ext. 5442 or by e-mail at MacmillanSpecialMarkets@macmillan.com.

Library of Congress Cataloging-in-Publication Data is available.

ISBN 978-1-250-10193-8

Book design by Eileen Savage
Feiwel and Friends logo designed by Filomena Tuosto
First Edition—2017

The artwork was created in Corel Painter using a "digital" piece of soft vine charcoal to draw
the black lines and paint the colors. Final color paintings were exported to Adobe Photoshop
and page layout was done in InDesign.

1 3 5 7 9 10 8 6 4 2

mackids.com

Motor Goose
Rhymes That Go!

poems by **Rebecca Colby**   illustrated by **Jef Kaminsky**

Feiwel and Friends
New York

Little Jack Junker

(Little Jack Horner)

Little Jack Junker,
broken-down clunker,
surprised all the cars
in the race.

'Cause right from the start,
he lost part after part,
yet he finished the race
in first place.

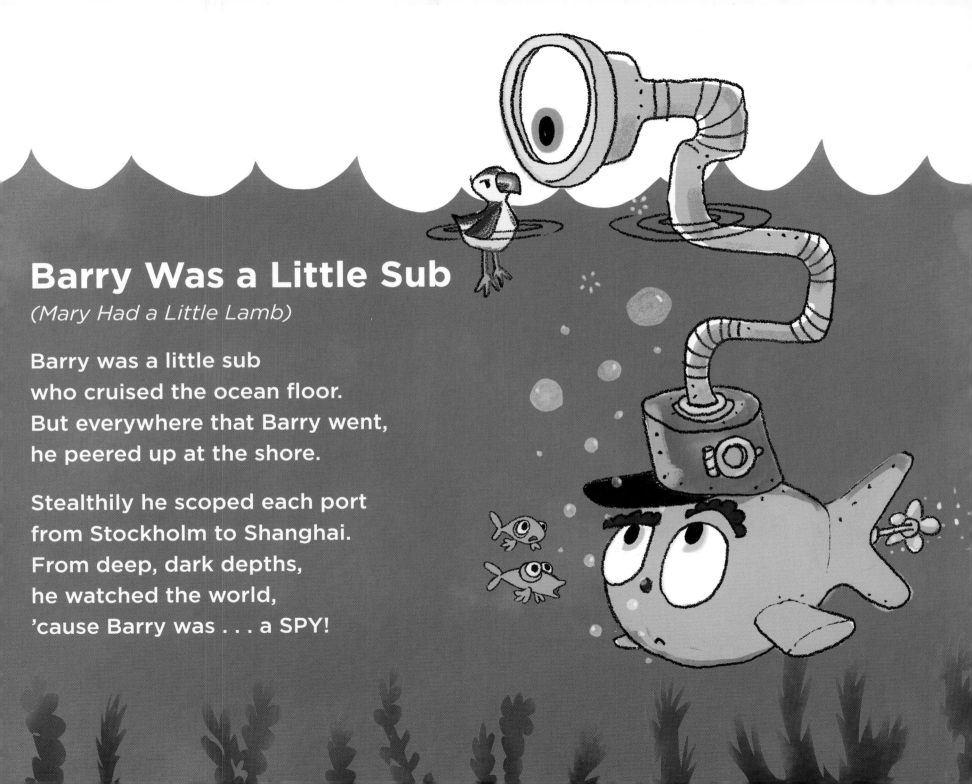

Barry Was a Little Sub
(Mary Had a Little Lamb)

Barry was a little sub
who cruised the ocean floor.
But everywhere that Barry went,
he peered up at the shore.

Stealthily he scoped each port
from Stockholm to Shanghai.
From deep, dark depths,
he watched the world,
'cause Barry was . . . a SPY!

Tow, Tow, Tow the Car

(Row, Row, Row Your Boat)

Tow, tow, tow the car,
slowly down the lane.
If it doesn't want to budge,
try a stronger chain.

Tow, tow, tow the car,
careful with your load.
Stop it swerving side to side.
Keep it on the road!

Mower Mary
(Mistress Mary, Quite Contrary)

Mower Mary, on the prairie,
how do you trim your field?
Hour by hour, with engine power,
and blades beneath my shield.

Swoopy-Loopy Airplane

(Itsy Bitsy Spider)

The swoopy-loopy airplane
flew high above the ground.
Down dived his nose
as he spiraled 'round and 'round.
Up swung his wingtips,
and he began to soar.
Then the swoopy-loopy airplane
flew higher than before.

Little Miss Mixer

(Little Miss Muffet)

Little Miss Mixer,
construction-site fixer,
poured concrete wherever she went.

Till along came a roller
who bowled her right over
and flattened her into cement.

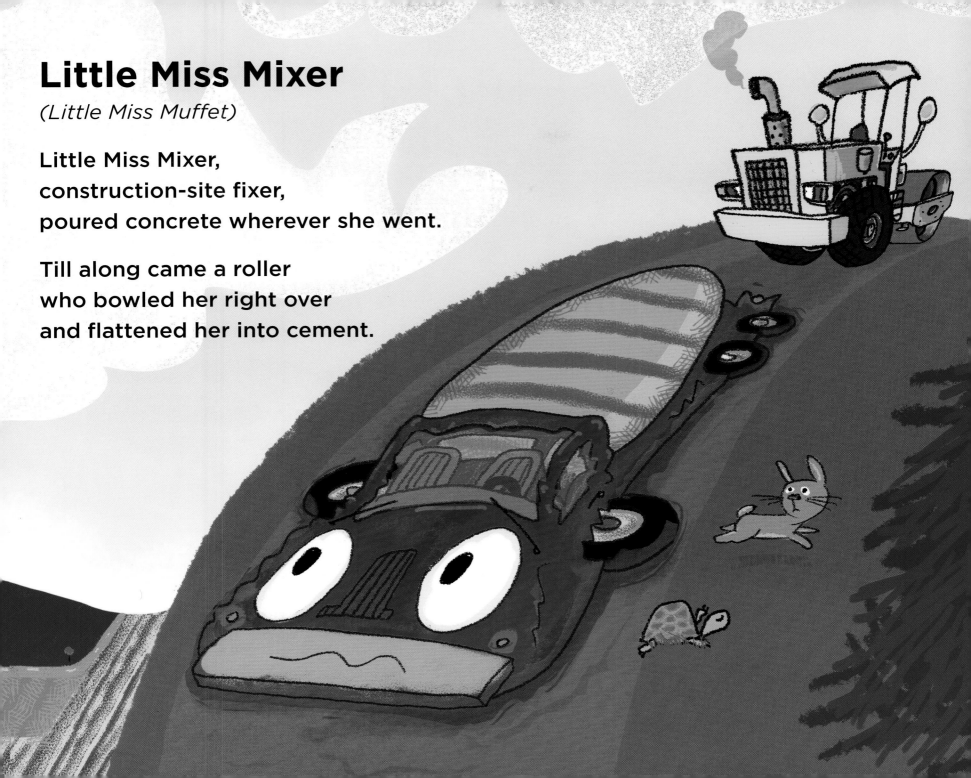

This Little Steam Train

(This Little Piggy)

This little steam train
climbed a mountain.
This little steam train
didn't roam.
This little steam train
had passengers.
This little steam train
had none.
And this little steam train whistled,
"Whoo, whoo, whoo!"
all the way home.

Bumpty Dumpty

(Humpty Dumpty)

Bumpty Dumpty picked up the trash,
Bumpty Dumpty had a big crash.
All the collectors and all the trashmen
gathered the garbage all over again.

Hey, Digger, Digger

(Hey, Diddle, Diddle)

Hey, digger, digger,
the hole's getting bigger.
Your shovel's been scooping since ten.
Beware the loose rubble.
Too late—you're in trouble!
You'd better start digging again.

Coach and Car

(Jack and Jill)

Coach and car both traveled far
to drive beside the sea.
But they got stuck—caught fast in muck—
till tow truck pulled them free.

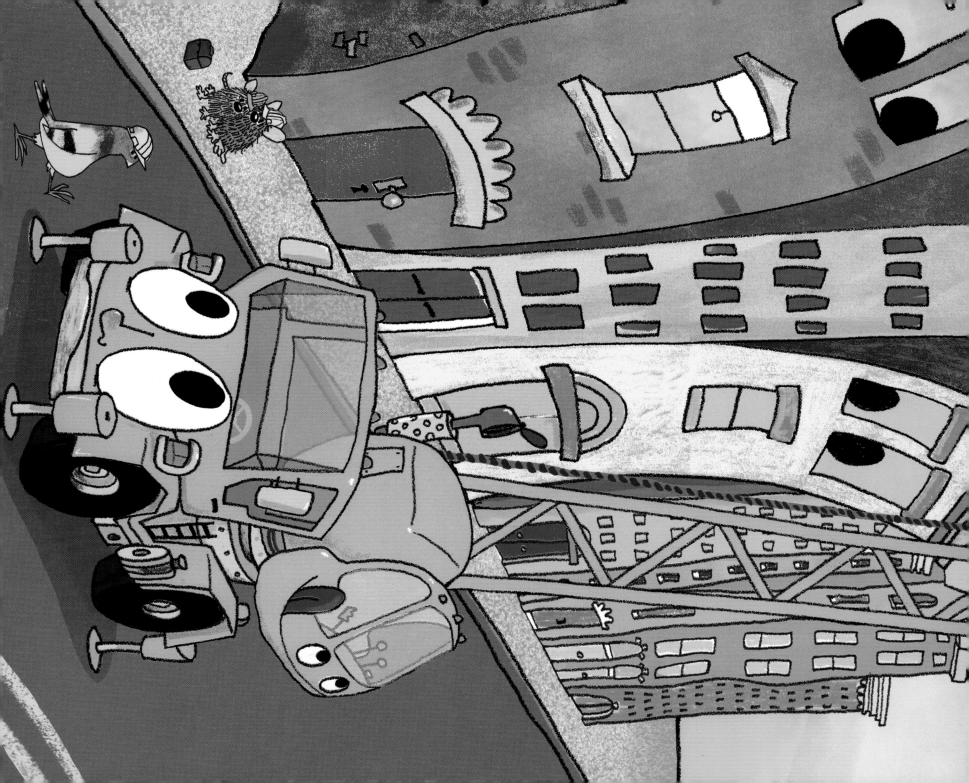

Crane Swing Steady
(Jack Be Nimble)

Crane swing steady,
crane swing fast,
crane knock over
the building mast.

Dirty Chopper

(Doctor Foster)

Dirty chopper, crop-dust hopper,
hovered above the plain.
He dusted for days,
in the grime and thick haze,
and never got clean again.

It's Clunking, It's Quaking

(It's Raining, It's Pouring)

It's clunking, it's quaking,
the muffler is shaking.
It spit and coughed out black exhaust,
and now it's finally breaking.

One, Two, Signal the Crew

(One, Two, Buckle My Shoe)

One, two,
signal the crew;
three, four,
engines roar;
five, six,
flick a switch;
seven, eight,
lift the freight;
nine, ten,
do it again.

Old Beat-Up Banger

(Old Mother Hubbard)

Old Beat-Up Banger
stalled in a hangar
while sheltering out of the rain.
Since he was there,
he made some repairs,
and now the old car is a plane.

London Bus Is Driving 'Round

(London Bridge Is Falling Down)

London Bus is driving 'round,
driving 'round, driving 'round.
London Bus is driving 'round
on vacation.

He came to see the city sights,
city sights, city sights.
He came to see the city sights
on vacation.

All he saw were traffic jams,
traffic jams, traffic jams.
All he saw were traffic jams
on vacation.

Higgity Chiggity Chug
(Hickory Dickory Dock)

Higgity chiggity chug,
the boat began to tug.
Although not large,
he pulls a barge.
Higgity chiggity chug.

Fireboats Are Red

(Roses Are Red)

Fireboats are red,
police cars are blue.
If you need help,
they'll rescue you!

Beep, Beep, Black Jeep

(Baa, Baa, Black Sheep)

Beep, beep, black jeep,
have you any gas?
Yes, car, yes,
it helped me pass.
One going uphill,
one pulling grain,
one pushing gravel,
working in the lane.

Roaring Rocket

(Yankee Doodle)

Roaring Rocket whizzed to Pluto,
with her turbo blaster.
There she spied a silver ship
that whizzed 'round even faster.

Roaring Rocket can't keep up.
Roaring Rocket's slowing.
Hurry! Tail those aliens
and find out where they're going!

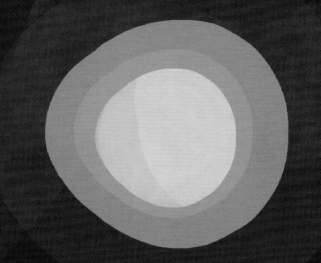

Twinkle, Twinkle, UFO

(Twinkle, Twinkle, Little Star)

Twinkle, twinkle, UFO,
how I wonder where you go.
Zipping past the Milky Way,
is your planet far away?
Twinkle, twinkle, UFO,
how I wonder where you go!

There Was an Old Taxi Who Parked in a Shed

(There Was an Old Woman Who Lived in a Shoe)

There was an old taxi who parked in a shed;
her tires were flat from the nails in her tread.
So she plugged them and patched them and
plumped them so fat,
that—POP! POP! POP! POP!—they once more went flat.

Rest Awhile, Cruiser

(Rock-a-Bye Baby)

Rest awhile, cruiser, in the garage.
When the day's through, it's time to recharge.
Shut down your engine, switch off each light,
turn off your siren and sleep through the night.